Our Best Friend's Littl[e]
A Billionaire MFM Rom[ance]

By Anastasia Slash

Follow Anastasia

[Join Anastasia Slash's mailing list for updates here!](#)

Copyright @ 2017 By Anastasia Slash all rights reserved.

[Follow Anastasia](#)

[STALK Anastasia CLICK HERE](#)

Publisher's note: this is a work of fiction. Names locations characters are a product of the author's imagination. Any resemblance to anyone is purely coincidental. Any resemblance to anybody living or dead, actual events or organizations is coincidental.

Other stories by Anastasia Slash you would enjoy

Claimed by my best friend's billionaire dad

Knocked up by the A List

Off Limits daddy

Taken by three billionaires

TITLES AND MEGA BUNDLES we love!

Hot thing boss

Billionaire daddy pop

Virgin curves for the billionaire

Sugar walls

Do Me Forever Baby

Parade's Kiss

Thunder

Creamed The Virgin

Reign On Me

Mr Goodnight's Package

B Prince Megabundle six books in one

Chapter 1 Megyn

It's late in the afternoon.

I found myself taking a break from studying for my midterms and daydreaming about my brother's toned, tall and sexy tattooed billionaire best friends and how I would love to have their massive cocks buried balls deep in my virgin pussy, when suddenly my phone started buzzing.

I picked up the call; it was my brother Jason.

We have not spoken in weeks, ever since he's started working on his brilliant startup.

He said "Hey little sis how are you doing? Listen I have a favor to ask."

I found it hilarious that even though I am 19, he still called me "little sis."

I said "Hey bro, what's the favor?"

"Hunter and Shane are going to be in your neck of the woods. They will be there for a conference. I figured they could check up on you."

Excited, my heart skipped a beat at that moment.

Hunter and Shane are my brother's gorgeous identical twin best friends.

I have had a freaking crush on both of them "like in forever," ever since they became best friends with my older brother Jason.

You see, Jason is five years older than me.

Jason would not allow me to get anywhere near his handsome friends; he felt they were bad boys. Or at least that's what Jason made me believe.

Back then he said, "You need to stay away from those guys, they are no good for you sis."

To make matters worse, each time I stepped into his room when the sexy brothers came visiting,

Jason would find a way to get me out of their presence.

"Hey can't we even talk to your sister? We, don't fucking bite," Hunter the older twin would say the minute I stepped out the room.

Then I would hear my brother's booming voice respond, "I don't care! You guys are not allowed to talk to Megyn unless I say so, which by the way is never. I know what you two are all about."

So today's call from Jason came as a surprise. I could not believe that Jason would tell me my sexy crushes are in town for a conference.

Now let me tell you a little bit about my brother's sexy, handsome best friends who used to be off-limits.

Hunter, he's the older one. He's bold and confident. He looks like an American male model who stepped out of a Ralph Lauren catalog. Tall, tanned and all muscle, he stands at 6 ft 6 inches tall with full sleeve tattoos and washboard abs.

He had piercing dark eyes, a natural tan, and gorgeous hair.

He was also brilliant in his way. Harvard educated thanks to their large trust fund account. But he left that behind, then he founded a company and sold it for a gazillion dollars! He was also a playboy, if you believe the tabloids.

But I got wet just thinking about him.

Shane, on the other hand, was the quiet one. I could never really understand why he stayed in Hunter's shadows. He too was Harvard educated, stunning and identical to Hunter. The only exception was the position of his sleeve tattoo. He preferred his symbol on the opposite arm.

The main difference between both sexy hunks was the color of their eyes. Shane had gorgeous blue eyes. Just the thought of having both of them sliding their massive cocks into my tight virgin pussy made my arousal grow.

I couldn't think straight picturing their hard spunk filled throbbing member spearing deep into my untouched wet slit.

"Are you there sis?" I heard Jason's voice jolt me back to reality.

I said, "yes I'm here that sounds exciting."

He paused for a moment and said, "They are there for a conference to meet some Silicon Valley investors. I asked they check on you to make sure no one's messing with my little sister."

"That's great! So you guys are finally doing this? You are raising money?" I asked changing the subject and happy to hear about my brother's startup.

Jason replied, "Yes hopefully it works out and then sis, we are off to a life of luxury."

I always wondered why Jason never asked Hunter or Shane for startup cash. Afterall they could afford it.

I guess he had a lot of pride in him why ask is best friends for money for the startup? He merely made them partners and if everything works out, everyone would get paid.

"I have to go now, sis. I have some meetings to attend. I'll probably join you later on sometime this week I'm not sure, but I'll let you know. They should be calling you I gave them your number, so maybe they will send you a text," Jason said.

I said, "That's fine bro; I'm looking forward to seeing them again."
Jason said, " I trust you, sis, remember they are still bad guys!"

I said " Don't worry, I will introduce them to Karla, my roommate. She likes bad boys."

I lied to my brother. I had no freaking intentions of introducing my sexy crushes to my roommate. I planned on keeping them to myself. I mean when next would I have this opportunity.

I hung up the line and stared between my legs; my pussy was soaked and throbbing picturing the moment, I would get to see them again.

Just then I got a text.

Hi, Megyn, it's Hunter, I'm just closing up on some meetings with investors. I'm sure your brother mentioned we are in town. I would like to see you tonight. Text your address. H

I shrieked in excitement. My dream come fucking true! I laid on my back and slid my fingers between my wet folds. Luckily Karla had classes at the time, so I was all alone which worked out fine because I needed my release. Hmm, I moaned sliding my fingers, parting my intimate folds.

"Oh yes, Hunter give me that massive throbbing cock of yours, slide it into my untouched pussy. I am so wet for you, darling. Shane, hmm let me flick my tongue over your smooth, delicious cockhead hmm, oh!'

I pinched my nipples with my left hand while my right worked my pulsating clit and my wet folds.

"Oh yes fuck yes, there" I moaned as my orgasm hit in shuddering waves. "Yes yes yes!" I cried out in pure bliss!

I smiled quivering as I returned to reality. Hell, I needed that release.

I always climaxed to the same dream every night. I pictured Hunter and Shane, taking turns with me.

Just then Karla walked in, she took a look at me and said "Are you okay?"
I said, "yes just had a fantasy that is all."
"Okay, easy with the fantasy girl. Guess what? we are going to a masked ball tonight!"

"No way, you got the invite?" I asked.

"Yeah, so get dressed," she commanded.

"Yeah, just give me a second, I need to send a text," I said holding my cell phone.

Karla grabbed the phone out of my hands and said: "Look we have to go you can text whoever it is, later. This a big event, so hurry girl."

I'll be honest, I've never been to a masked ball before. I was excited as we got dressed and headed out.

Honestly, I felt awkward in the tight bodycon dress, Karla insisted that it was the perfect outfit for me. She said, "You are going to find yourself a hot handsome guy to take home."

I shrugged and said "I'm not exactly trying to meet anyone, Karla!"

That is the moment I remembered; I did not text Hunter.

I said, "Oh no I forgot to send the text to Hunter, my brother's friend."

She said, "forget about him for now, let's just have some fun."

I had no choice but to agree with her and got dressed. Then we headed out to the event. We got to the mansion it was gorgeous, ten bedrooms and six bathrooms. I marveled at the sight before me.

A home this massive in Silicon Valley can cost upwards of $10 million. At least. She looked at me and said, "Why, lady, you look as though you seen a freaking ghost?"

I said, "I was not exactly expecting to see such an edifice. I mean why exactly are we here?"

"Seriously, why are we here? We are here to have fun, that's all," Karla replied

" I'm sorry I just feel a little out of place right," I said.

She said: "Don't worry about it it's going to be okay."

I said, "Alright" Then I watched as she handed the invitation to the bouncer at the door.

He looked at us. Then he gave us two Golden female masks and ushered us into the luxurious home.

"See I told you. That bouncer dude likes us, especially you," Karla said laughing. Then she said well the rules are that we have to put on these masks.

Chapter 2 Shane

Usually, Hunter would attend these boring investor meetings alone. But this particular silicon valley investor with amaze ventures was adamant about my being there as well, fucking hell. Luckily the whole ordeal did finally come to an end hours later!

"We will continue this some other time" Byron Myers the Amaze Ventures Capitalist dude said. We shook his hand and adjourned for the freaking night.

As we walked out the building, I noticed it was already 10 pm.

I glanced at Hunter once the meeting ended and said: "Whew that's a fucking relief, bro!"

Hunter laughed and said "You got that right, Shane. Now it's time for some fun, yeah!"

I turned to my brother as we got into our Mercedes Maybach and said: "Say, have you heard back from Megyn yet?"

He shook his head and said, "I haven't heard a word."

"That is unlike her; I hope she is doing okay," I said.

Hunter shrugged. Then he said turning on the ignition, "She is probably out there pleased to be away from Jason's clutches!"

We burst out laughing.

Jason fucking kept Megyn under some strict rules. None of his friends were allowed to talk to her without his permission.

It's seemed ridiculous then, and it seems insane now.

When we first asked about her, he refused to give us her number! I mean what are we going to do? Then again if she wants us, we would love to please her. The thought of my long thick cock dipping into her tight wet slit, made my dick twitch. "Down boy!" I murmured adjusting my erection.

Jason thought about it when I reminded him Stanford had a lot of spoilt, entitled lousy trust fund frat boys, ready to take his sweet Megyn for a naughty ride. That made him change his mind in an instant.

"Yeah, to be honest, I was quite surprised he listened to us,"I said to Hunter: "Well since you haven't heard back from her maybe we should go ahead with Plan B?" I argued.

Hunter looked at me and said, "Perhaps we should give her a few more minutes?"

"Okay," I said.

This time I tried texting her but still no response.

"Fucking hell, I really would like to see her. I know you do too, don't lie," Hunter said.

I looked at my brother and said "Of course I do, that should not be a question. But does she want to see us?"

"Well, she is still not responding so maybe the answer is no?"

Hunter said. "I guess you're right, let's go with Plan B. Let's head over to the masquerade ball."

Alright, bro," And with that Hunter steered the car towards the mansion.

Then he said, "I think we should head out to the hotel to change first? What do you say?"

I replied:"I don't think that's necessary I think we're okay as we are. Besides, it's going to be incredible; we always have the ladies lining up for us!"

Hunter was always the one who cared more about his style.

I could care less.

I was more of the outdoorsy type.

But then Hunter insisted. He said "If we are going to make a good impression on the possible investors at this party. We might as well look incredible tonight. I'll make a call."

And with that Hunter called our style concierge in the area.

The guy said, "Right away sir. The designer will have your bespoke suits ready in 10 minutes sir."

"Good," Hunter said. Then he shot me a look and said:"The perks of being well-heeled!"

I arched an eyebrow back at him and said, "Of course, I never doubted that for a second."

We made a quick stop over at the British designer Eton's home. He was super excited to see us and quickly gave us our designer suits.

And to top it off he said "here. I made these masks especially for you. No one else would have the same one."

We thanked him, got dressed and got back into our vehicle. It didn't take long to arrive at the mansion. Alan, the guy hosting the party, was one of our favorites go to investors and an old friend. We all knew what kind of event he had planned.

It happened to be a private sex party.

"Well well well looks like he outdid himself again. Floodlights and everything," Hunter said as we stepped out the car and walked straight into the building. We picked up a couple of drinks here and there noticing the beautiful, enticing masked women, thinking which one's pussy will feel snug as she cums around our cocks.

Then I noticed her, a beauty to behold standing there with her gorgeous curvy body and large suckable ample tits. My cock twitched at that moment. Hunter's dick had the same reaction too. I whispered to Hunter: "Isn't she gorgeous over there. so fuckable"

Hunter kept gaze on her he said "fuck yeah she's gorgeous, large tits and curves to die for. Fuck, I've never seen anyone that beautiful. you know what she actually reminds me of..."

Then he paused, as though realizing what he was about to say.

I looked at him and said, "she reminds you of Megyn, right?"

"Yeah," he said.

Then Hunter continued, "damn these masked rules. That angel is seriously fuckable in the right way. She's gorgeous she has perfect sized tits and an ass that goes around. Oh my god that ass."

"Too bad we're not allowed to say our names, but I guess that's a good thing," I said.

"Well," Hunter said, "if we can't be with Megyn, I'll say that curvaceous model over there will do just fine, we can pretend she is our sweet innocent Megyn," Hunter said smiling at the masked beauty. I smiled at her too; then we made our move towards her.

Chapter 3 Megyn

I was a fidgety mess.

I kept looking around at the utterly naked couples with only masks on pleasuring themselves. I said to Karla: "This is no ordinary party. It looks like a sex party."

She laughed and said,"And? of course, it is. You need to get laid. You need someone to pop that cherry, and that's why we're here."

I said to her "This was not exactly what I had in mind."

She laughed. Then I said, "but I'll be honest watching everybody do it it seems so natural and beautiful."

She laughed and said "Look at that contraption over there the little clamps wouldn't you like that on your nipples"

I stared at the sex harness contraption with shocked eyes and said, "No I really wouldn't."

She laughed and said: "Well this is where we part ways."

I stared at her with wide eyes and exclaimed, "Freaking hell you're not going to leave all alone!"

She laughed and said "I see someone who needs my help, that hot masked man behind the bar!"

And with that she walked over to the bar and slid down on her knees.

I watched as Karla knelt before this gorgeous sexy masked hunk and unbuckled his pants. I stared, as his thick throbbing cock fell gently into the palm of her hands.

Then she slid her lips over his glistening crown and began sucking his entire shaft into her mouth.

I must admit I got freaking aroused just staring at them. At first, I didn't notice two handsome masked strangers staring at me.

Then I turned, and our eyes met. Both looked at me and whispered something to one another. I bit my lip suggestively loving the attention. Filled with lust, I felt my pussy clench. Perhaps Karla was right; maybe it is time to pop my cherry.

Then they made their way towards me. The positioned their bodies next to mine watching Karla in action.

They said, "Your friend is doing it the right way. The way she is flicking her tongue around his cock is perfect."

I smiled mesmerized by their enticing fragrance and their sexy masculine body.

I swear, their perfume was a freaking natural aphrodisiac. My juices began trickling down my legs. I had to slide my thighs together in a bid to stop my nectar from hitting the floor.

I was so turned on by both men; my heart began to race.

Then I felt a hand glide down my waist and massage my ass.

I stayed still and gasped in pleasure. I loved this man's firm hand on my behind.

He said "We are identical twins but per the rules, no names. But I am not the quiet twin. We want to please you."

I didn't respond. Instead, I pushed my ass back towards my masked confident lover's hand.

He smiled and purred, "Hmm, Good girl you like that? You are very naughty, aren't you?"

I got soaked just thinking about what they were going to do to me. The quiet twin slid in front of me, while the not so quiet one slipped behind me. Both sexy hunks' bodies effectively sandwiched mine.

I felt beautiful as the one in front kissed me on the nape of my neck, while the other one behind pushed to speak cock between my ass cheeks while still massaging them. I leaned backward and squeezed the masked one behind my ass's cock, listening as he hissed "Hmm yeah, nice ass darling!"

Then he murmured capturing my ear in his lips " We are going to take you to the private sex room.

The purple room, sweetie. You are going to cum all night long until you see a higher being. We want to feel your pussy cum around our cock, will you like that?"

I only nodded as little gasps of pleasure escaped my lips. I felt a mix of excitement and worry, but I was also aroused and wet, my body wanted to experience everything they had planned. Without saying another word they led me to the purple sex room.

I thought I seen crazy things before this was insane.

There were floggers & spanking paddles. It was like something I'd seen in a movie, what was that called again? " Some Shades" movie. But this time it was my reality.

The quiet one whispered while the other stepped aside, "Don't worry we don't need a lot of tools to get you wet and begging for more, we will just take our time to ensure you're delighted because that's what we do."

"Hmm, Can I taste you darling?" He murmured.

Before I could respond, he placed his hands underneath my behind, lifted me up and placed me on the pleasure swing.

He sunk down to his knees and spread my legs apart. My tiny barely covered virgin pussy, got exposed for his pleasure.

His masked brother held the swing in place with one hand and began kneading my ample boobs with the other. I watched as the quiet one flicked his fingers sensually between my inner thighs moving up until his hand palmed my wet throbbing pussy.

"Hmm so wet already, I need a drink, sweetie." He murmured snapping my thong off. Then he flicked the tip of his magic tongue up and down my wet folds. I moaned pushing my hips towards him. My drenched curls tickled his nose.

"Tastes incredible like ice cream baby." He purred licking and sucking on my nub. Then he said "God, you are fucking beautiful."

By now the other hunk had pulled out my large ample breasts. He began pinching my nipples, alternating between the right and the left breasts." I was a panting mess, their actions sent my body reeling to the arms of ecstasy. I wanted to taste him. I fumbled with his pants until his pulsating massive cock sprang out into my awaiting hands. Then he took his hand off my breast and proceeded to hang on to the swing keeping it in place, while I fisted his cock and flicked my tongue of his precum glistening tip.

"Fuck yeah!" he groaned as my I slid my lips over his entire length until he was in my wet core balls deep. I placed my left hand underneath is cock and teased his balls. Then I began bopping my head back and forth over his shaft. I slid my tongue over the ridges from the base to the tip and then I continued sucking on him like a lollipop.

I gasped and writhed my waist as the quiet one's tongue speared deep into my dripping wet sex. His tongue slid out my wet slit, I groaned: "please feels so good, don't stop, I beg you!"

Without a word he replaced his tongue with a finger, then another into my dripping hole. He pumped his fingers inside my core pulling my body into an intense shuddering orgasm. I cried in pleasure, content from the reality of having my two gorgeous men pleasuring me.

I imagined were Shane and Hunter brought my body to a shuddering climax. I felt relaxed as the confident one lifted me off the swing and placed me on the large four poster bed.

"Would you like to try something new darling?" The confident one asked holding onto a nylon silk scarf. I thought about it for a moment and thought why not. "Yes" I purred

He smiled and lowered my back on the bed. Then he took my right hand and tied my hand to the bed frame with the scarf. The quiet one did the same with the left.

"We want you to feel pleasure darling, we please you and have your snug pussy clenching hard on our pulsating cocks."

"First the feather darling," the confident one continued, sliding a delicate feather over my trembling curves. Then he slid his fingers from my feet up my inner thighs until his hand palmed my manicured wet mound. My intimate curls glistened in his hands coating them with my wetness.

"Hmm you are ready,"

"Wait... I said pushing my chest up. The quiet one slipped his lips delicately over my sensitive nipples making me moan and arch up my back as far as it would go.

"I am a virgin..." I blurted out without thinking. I looked at my masked lovers, a smile crept up on both their faces.

"Hmm don't worry darling we will be gentle," The quiet one spoke up moving up and positioning his body between my thighs. I watched as he stroked his cock up and slid it between my legs nudging at my entrance. The confident one locked his lips on mine parting my lips with his tongue. He murmured "relax you are gorgeous, and you deserve to be worshipped darling. Please let us take care of you babe!"

That is the moment I heard the quiet one whisper "Spread your gorgeous legs darling."
I did as he requested. My breathing increased in anticipation. The confident one kept kissing my lips then he slid his fingers down on my clit and began drawing circles on my throbbing sensitive nub.

Then I felt pressure at my entrance, I looked down with hooded lens as the quiet one thrust an inch of his huge long cock into my tight wet virgin pussy.

"Ohh hmmm," I gasped pulling back as his girth stretch sliding into my sex but he placed his arm around me and held me in place. He whispered in a soft voice: "Darling don't fight it, let me in sweetie. God, You are so beautiful, so fucking tight like a glove, feels so good fuck! hmm,I want to experience this moment with you darling!" Once I heard those words I opened up for him like a flower, as his thick girth stretched open my virgin walls. Then I heard a popping sound as his cock moved past by virgin barrier. I was so wet, I did not feel any pain just pressure.

Soon that pressure turned to ultimate pleasure. The confident one got up and left the quiet one and me alone. I felt a sensual friction as he thrust his large throbbing spunk filled member between my thighs into my sex. He lowered his lips on my ear and began talking dirty "Fuck, you are so fucking tight. I love moving inside your royal pussy. Feels so good, like a tight glove baby. Thank you sweetheart"

His hands fingers caressed my Clit as he pounded his way deep inside my tight wet walls. My pussy muscles clenched hard on his veiny shaft as it speared through my soaked core sending jolts of pleasurable sensations through my entire body.

He held me close as our bodies moved in rhythm with each other.

"Oh there, hmm, I am cumming!" I cried out staring into his eyes and wrapping my legs around his hips.

"Come darling! Come!" he commanding pounding his hardness faster and harder into my pulsating soaked tight pussy. I felt my body explode at that moment as an overwhelming climax came in shuddering waves.

"Hmm," I cried out in ecstasy, tugging at my wrists spiraling down into a drained state, still at his mercy as he slammed his fully seated entire length in and out my slippery tight hole. I watched as he desperately sought his climax. He gripped my waist. The he cried out and began to shudder as my intimate muscles clenched around his cock milking him.

"Fuck you feel so good baby, here I cum darling!" His face looked so beautiful I could not look away as he surged inside me letting out a growl of pleasure releasing ropes of his creamy cum inside my spent pussy.

Spent and smiling with pleasure, the quiet one stared down between my legs as my juices mixed with his cum slid down soaking up the sheets.

He lowered his lips to mine and kissed me. It was a wet and possessive kiss. The quiet one slid his cock out of me and released my wrists from the bed frame. Then the confident one positioned his body between my juice dripping thighs.

"Now you are ready for me darling" he groaned nudging his spunk filled member at my entrance. I felt the tip of his swollen dick rubbing against my pussy as he slicked it up and down my wetness. "Fuck he is so big" I moaned turning in my head to side as his large girth sunk its way deep into my soaked newly popped wet hole. My pussy clenched on pulsating hardness as it thrust deeper and deeper into my soaking wet pussy. My juices trailed down the sheets of the bed. Then all of a sudden, he flipped me over, his back was now on the bed and I on top. The sounds of his rock hard cock slamming up into my desperate hole made me come over and over again.

"Fuck babe, you are incredible darling," he murmured thrusting his hips up and grabbing my breasts. "We are here for you darling, all for you angel."

I was in ecstasy, his dirty talk drove me wild with passion.

"Fuck i love your body darling, I love how soft your sexy body is darling, nngh" he grunted slamming up into me. Then he placed his arms around my waist and lowered my body down on his chest. That is the moment I heard the sound of the quiet one stroking lube on his cock. I turned to look at him it made its way to us my eyes widened, he murmured " darling would you like to try something yeah back here?"

He said massaging my ass as he spread my ass cheeks apart, and ran the finger around my ass. He slid a finger into my derriere. I bucked my hips back to let him know I want more.

He lowered his lips to my ear and said "I want to fuck you here darling relax baby"

The he slid his thick hardness inch by inch into my tight ass, pausing to let allow my body adjust to his thick shaft. The confident one did not stop thrusting his length up my dripping wet walls.

"Don't stop keep on, if feels so good," I moaned.

I felt pressure but soon he continued pushing deeper and then the pressure I felt turned to incredible pleasure. Our sweat filled bodies began moving in rhythm with each other as one.

Chapter 4 Hunter

We were in the throes of fucking and pleasuring her, my cock loved the feeling of her tight wet virgin pussy. Then I noticed a heart tattoo right before her bikini line. Fucking hell! I thought.

I looked up at Shane who was happily sliding his cock in and out her beautiful ass. He looked back at me as he grabbed handfuls of her massive tits from behind as he slammed into her tight puckered lips.

Our sexy masked babe had her eyes closed, caught up in the wave of passion.

I murmured to Shane, "Megyn?"

A broad smile came across Shane's face once he realized it was our dream girl, Megyn! He slid his cock almost entirely out of her tight ass, she groaned:

"No please," she cried. "I love the feeling of both of your cocks filling me up, please don't pull out."
Shane felt a little guilty about our little secret. But then the reality that we were fucking our dream girl made whatever reservations he had disappear in an instant!

He slicked his cock around her ass ring and nudged his cock at her back entrance, then he grabbed her by the hips and slammed his entire length back into her tight back wall until his balls began slapping her ass.

I kept on fucking her tight wet tiny hole as it clenched on my shaft. I could barely breathe. She was so fucking snug, just like a freaking glove. It was a good thing I let Shane go in first before me. I grabbed her giant tits and began sucking her nipples as I thrust my cock up into her wet dripping walls.

"I want us to fucking come together baby, would you like that hmm?"

Fuck Megyn's snug slit was the best I have ever had.

In the past, I stayed away from virgins because they get too emotional after sex. They wanted more than I can offer. But fuck it, there was no way; I was going to pull out of her tight walls. So

I kept pumping my hardness up into her core, watching as her breasts bounced up and down in front of my face. I sat up and squeezed each one. Then I flicked my tongue on her right nipple, and then the left. Soon I began alternating between them. Fucking her tight hole and sucking her boobs, while Shane kept the pace taking her from behind.

She couldn't take it much longer. She cried out between loud moans:

"Ohh, hmm here I come here. I am fucking cumming. I can't hold back any longer."

"Hmm darling god you are gushing all over sweetie, good girl."

The sound of her cries made us increase the pace of our hard thrusts. We continued slamming our cocks into her pussy and her ass until Shane, and I also felt our bodies shudder.

"I am going to cum inside you too," I cried out. "I want you to have our baby!"

Shane and I wrapped our hands around her petite body. We each gave her one final savage thrust. Watching her scream in ecstasy as cums drove us mad we shot every last drop of our creamy load into her.

Spent, Shane pulled his cock out of her ass and fell over to the side of the bed while I lifted her up off my cock and lowered her body between us. I wanted to pull these fucking masks off, but I decided to keep it on.

Plus I was tired and could barely keep my eyes open.

When we woke up, she was gone.

She left.

I took that damn mask off my face. I said to Shane "Fucking hell, I hope she will call us. I cannot believe she left."

We rose to our feet and got dressed. Then we walked out the mansion without saying a word to the host, Alan.

Shane said as we got seated in the car: "She was fucking hot, God everything about her was so tight."

" Well, I guess we better head out to our hotel," I said turning on the car's ignition. "Yes," Shane agreed. We headed back to our Penthouse suite and called it a night.

The following morning we heard a loud knock on our door. Then a familiar voice said: "Open the fucking door."

We recognized the voice immediately; it was Jason's.
Why would he be at our door so fucking early in the morning? Then I glanced at the clock it wasn't morning it was noon. Then I realized we had missed our appointment with the investor.

I put on a robe and opened the door. Jason took one look at me and growled: "Where were you guys all night?"

I looked to Jason and said, "Out, and we weren't expecting you to come to town we were handling it."

He said "What exactly were you handling? Because you fucking missed the appointment with Amazing Adventures today. How am I going to get the startup funded if my partners keep screwing things up? Then he paused and swallowed.

He said "I was over at my sister's place this morning after the meeting and I saw this. Hunter, is this yours?" he growled holding up my favorite designer bracelet.

I couldn't believe Megyn took It. I wondered where it was. I had to deny everything. I lied: "It is not mine. We haven't even seen your sister yet."

Shane looked away and didn't say anything.

That the moment, Jason said "You better not be fucking my virgin sister, I mean it. Get your clothes now, the two of you and let's head over to another meeting before all hell breaks loose and we lose everything we've worked so hard for this past year!"

He tossed the bracelet into my hands and walked out. We got dressed and headed out to the meeting.

Chapter 5   Megyn

A couple of weeks went by, and it seemed as though Jason and his friends had decided to extend their stay.

I still haven't gotten a chance to see Hunter or Shane yet.

 Once Jason came to town and saw my souvenir from the masked party he forbade me from seeing them, I wonder why. Maybe he thought I would sleep with them if given a chance.

I didn't tell him I got the bracelet from a sex party and lost my virginity to two masked lovers. He said the band looked like Hunters!

For some reason, I have been feeling a little nauseous lately.

Karla noticed she said, "You need to see a doctor, you know it's not best for you to remain this way."

I said," I was fine."

But she insisted, she paused and blurted out: "Could you be pregnant?"

Shocked, I thought about her question for a moment and said "There's no way in hell, I could be pregnant or is there? I have not had sex with anyone else since the night of the party."

She folded her arms and said "Well, honestly you have all the symptoms. You know what I'm going to do? I'm going to get you a test right now." Then she continued: "Hmm, guess what? I have one available." she rummaged through her bag and whipped out a 3-minute pregnancy kit!

Surprised to see she had the test available, I asked: " How is it that you have one in your bag? Do you carry it everywhere?"

She laughed and said" Well you just never know! Now hurry! Take the test!"

With trembling hands, I grabbed the test from her. Then I made my way to the bathroom. I sat down on that toilet seat and took the test.

It felt like an eternity waiting for the results.

I bit my nails worried. *What if I'm pregnant?* I pondered.

"Which twin is the dad and who are they? My perfect twin strangers, will I ever see them again? Am I destined to be alone?" My knees quivered. I kept looking back at the test. Three minutes couldn't come fast enough. Finally, the lines showed up, and the test read: "Congrats! You are pregnant. I placed my palms on my lips!" Freaking hell, how will I break the news to Jason? I felt as though I'd let everyone down. I called out to Karla. She rushed right in and said, "Oh my, you're pregnant."

I looked up at her and said "You think?"

She gasped and said "So which one of the masked twins is the father? I know you have not had sex ever since!"

"I don't know which one is the father. God, I feel terrible for doing this, for getting carried away."

Karla then asked, "So what are you going to do?"

I shook my head and thought there goes my scholarship.

We stepped out of the bathroom.

I placed the test on my desk.

I told Karla "Not a word about this to anybody! Especially my brother."

She agreed and said, "It's our secret, I'll keep it safe. But whatever you decide, I will be there for you."

I nodded and swallowed, wondering what my life was going to entail, now that I'm expecting a child.

Just then we heard a knock on the door.

Karla opened it and gasped she said "Oh my god I know you! You are....."

It was Hunter.

He said " Everyone knows who I am. I am Megyn's brother's best friend. Can I speak with Megyn alone please?"

"Wow, you are "the Hunter?" One of the most eligible billionaires in the world? sure come on in!" Karla exclaimed.

I looked up pleased to see Hunter, but wondering why the sudden visit after all this time. Karla agreed and then she stepped out of the room.

Hunter hugged me, and we both sat on the couch.

I didn't know what to say.

I was happy to see him.

My arousal grew and my pussy clenched, just staring into his eyes.

Then my hand brushed the designer bracelet on his wrist. It was the same one, Jason took from me! I swallowed and thought: "Oh my God could it be?"

Could it be the twins I had sex with at the sex club were Hunter and Shane? I began trembling.

Hunter placed a tender arm around me and asked: "Are you okay?"

I whispered "yes" then my eyes darted back down to his Designer Bracelet. He noticed.

He said, in a deep sexy voice: "You probably know, right?"
I said," Where you the one at the private party?Was that you and Shane with masks on?"
I kept rambling out questions hoping to hear the truth.

Hunter nodded and said, "Yes darling, it was Shane and me."

Hunter placed his hand lovingly on my thigh and held me close. He said "Megyn, sweetie, I came here to apologize. But being next to you, I can't help the way I feel."

His hands glided up my thighs and palmed my drenched mound. He said planting soft kisses on my neck, "Sweetie, I want you I need you please! Can you forgive me for not telling you that night?"

"Yes," I murmured, my sensitive nipples got hard in anticipation.

And with that he cupped my face and parted my lips with his magic tongue, thrusting it down my throat.

I kissed him back grabbing his hair.

Hunter placed his hands underneath my ass and pulled me closer to him.

I straddled my legs around his hips and watched as he rose to his feet and carried me until my back hit a wall. We were mad with desire, our lips never leaving the other. He slid his pants down and tore my thong off.

Then he fisted his thick cock and placed its glistening tip nudging my wet tight slit. My eyes fluttered shut ready in anticipation.

I was wet and ready to receive him. Then he teased my folds for a moment coating his tip with my wetness. I moaned and pleaded: "Please don't tease, I want to feel you inside my tight walls, please."

"Hmm, how badly do you want me, baby, cause I need you like I fucking need to breathe!" He groaned.

"Very badly, please" I begged.

Hunter said:" Say no more darling, I aim to please only you."
That is the moment he pressed his tip hard into my core.
"Jesus fuck you are so fucking tight and wet!"

He said thrusting his entire length balls deep into my tight wet slit. I closed my eyes as his veiny thick shaft stretched my pussy to its limit.

Overwhelmed with intense passion, Hunter placed his hands on my top and slid it down to my waist. My breasts ached with need begging for his sensual touch. My nipples grew hard as he thrust his cock up into my wet dripping hole.

He flicked his tongue over my sensitive nipples then closed his lips over it while his fingers worked my other breast. I became a panting freaking mess. I hoped the baby inside of me was Hunters; I loved his rough confident thrusts. My breasts bounced in his face.

"Your breasts tastes like heaven, I love your juice" He purred sucking my nipple and making me even more aroused. "Fuck yeah, I am addicted to your tight soft pussy darling." Then his mouth moved over to the other nipple and sucked greedily on it. I gasped with each measured thrust. My walls clenched hard on his thick girth.

"Oh there, there, I am cumming!" I cried out.

I couldn't hold back any longer; I teetered on the brink of ecstasy, then my body shuddered, bowing to an intense orgasm.

Hunter did not stop. His pulsating cock kept pounding in my wet slit, as it raced to an intense climax. He slammed his hardness faster and harder growling with pleasure until his cum erupted like a volcano up into my tight hole. I felt for sure it hit my cervix.

We were both panting as we stared into each other's eyes, we did not realize the door was open. That's is the moment Hunter felt a firm pair of hands grab him off me! I groaned as his cock slid out my pussy leaving it dripping white cream between my legs. Then I realized it was my brother, Jason's hands! Hell!

"What the fuck!" Jason cried out. "Not my sister!" He yelled punching Hunter. Hunter swung back.

I cried out in panic, "Jason, please stop! Please stop!"

I pleaded with Jason, but it was of no use he kept on hitting Hunter. I could tell Hunter was holding back from hurting Jason out of respect. Jason was no match for Hunter's size.

"Jesus man, I fucking love her man!" Hunter cried out. "I fucking love your sister."

Jason's eyes turned to the pregnancy test on the desk.

He looked at me still grabbing onto Hunter and fumed: "Are you fucking pregnant? Answer me, Megyn, what's this? He asked exasperatedly letting go of Hunter shirt. Then he grabbed the pregnancy test.

I turned and looked away. "Megyn, tell me are you, is this yours?" He asked once more.
With tears in my eyes, I admitted: "Yes I am."
He gasped:
"Get out he growled at his best friend. Get the fuck out!"

Hunter panting wanted to respond. But instead, he looked my way and said: "I will leave if she tells me to leave."

Then Hunter turned to Jason and said: "Jason, Shane and I love your sister. We always have and always will!"

"What the fuck! Are you saying Shane is also in on this too? Megyn?" Jason growled.

I turned looking away.
Then I turned to Hunter with tears in my eyes and murmured while avoiding his gaze: 'please go."
"You heard her go! Or we will fucking take this outside," Jason growled.

Hunter said stoically:

"That's okay I will leave, but I will be back. I love you, Megyn."

And with that Hunter turned and walked towards the door when just then, Shane walked in the room.

Jason glanced at Shane and yelled: "Shane... I want you out of my sister's dorm room right now. Both of you!"

Shane asked with widened eyes: "What's going on?"

"You know you both had your way with my sister, then I come here to find Hunter fucking Megyn! Well...congratulations you are going to be a dad!

But wait, Shane, no one knows whose baby it is! Yours or Hunters? You know what? Enough talk. Fucking get out of here right now."

Shane looked pale he wanted to respond, but Hunter held his hand and said:

"Come to one Shane let's go..."

Shane looked me in the eyes.

"Megyn is it true? Are you pregnant? Are you sweetie?" Shane asked in a soft voice.

Before I could respond, Jason pushed Shane and Hunter out the door and locked it.

"You cannot control my life forever. I love them!" I yelled at Jason.

"You will get over them. I promise." He said hugging me. "I want you to get your things. You are going home with me. You will have to transfer schools ."

"No!" I yelled sobbing.

Jason held me and said "I am just trying to protect you sis, that is all."

Chapter 6 Shane

"What the hell man what was that about?" I asked once we got in the car.

Hunter looked at me and said you know he found out about that night and caught Megyn and I. What's worse is, she's expecting a baby, our baby."

I replied in surprise: "Freaking hell Hunter, I love this girl I think she's the one for us."

Hunter said "It's not about her being the one Hunter, Jason would never allow it. I hope he wouldn't do anything to hurt Megyn or the startup because that would be the last straw."

"I don't think he'll do that I think he just needs to cool off. But hell I had a hard time leaving our Megyn behind. She should've come with us. Dammit. I don't care what Jason thinks."

Hunter looked out the window at that moment, then back on the road.

He said "Right now I am also worried about the possibility of losing our VC investments. I know we have enough personal funds to keep the startup going, but I really do not want Jason to pull out of the company."

Just then, a text came through on Shane's phone from Jason.

"Well looks like he already did," I said, looking at the text, it read:

"The deal is fucking off. I'm selling my shares to you two. You better pay up. I don't want anything to do with you guys!Stay away from my family, especially Megyn!"

Hunter sighed. Then, he said out loud: "Jason is always dramatic. Megyn is carrying our child. We will not stay away."

I agreed.

This wasn't the first time Jason had gotten mad at us. Looking back now he never wanted us to have anything to do with his sister. I mean even when Jason had a party at his home, he would hide Megyn away.

For some reason, he did everything possible to keep her away from us.

But we couldn't stay away from her, let's just say the party always ended with us getting kicked out by Jason. Back to reality,

Hunter said, "Well if that's the way he feels about it there's nothing we can do."
Then he changed his mind and said: "You know what I'm going to give him a call, let's see what happens."
We called Jason's number and yet again no response.
Hunter said, "I guess we will let things cool off but damn I'm not letting her go, are you?"

I looked at my twin and said "There is no way in hell, I would let her go. I love her; she's ours, that night was magical. I can't stop thinking about her. Plus she is having our baby!"

Hunter agreed. We decided to take a break. But weeks later, I couldn't hold back any longer. I yearned to be with her. I wanted to feel her cumming around my cock once more. But for the most part, I had to know how she felt about us.

I called her line, no response.

Then I sent her a text that read "are you thinking about me and as much as I'm thinking about you." I didn't expect a response right away, but I was pleasantly surprised and pleased to receive one moment later.

She wrote "I can't help it. I think about you every night and every day. I miss you too."

I sent another text:

Can we meet somewhere neutral to talk?

She replied saying she wished we could, but Jason wants her back home. He also convinced her to take the next semester off and transfer schools.

She then added : "I do not know what to do.'

I asked about the baby; she said the baby was healthy. She then texted: " We did a sonogram, and it's twins!"

I almost fell out of my chair at that moment; she had our twins. That's it I said to myself:" We are going back for her,"

I called Jason. For some reason, he picked up the call. I said: "You know what Jason you can have the company, we will give back your shares and ours. But Megyn is ours; we love her more than life itself."

Jason said "I don't care what you do. Fucking stay away from my sister."

I said I've always been the reasonable quiet twin, Jason. But you know how much Hunter and I love her so this shouldn't come as a surprise to you."

Jason said "I don't fucking care how you feel, Shane. This isn't about you; it is about my sister. Fuck your feelings."

I then said: "Jason, she is pregnant with our twins. Do whats right, see reason in this for crying out loud!"

Jason hung up before I could say another word.

I realized he was still upset, but it did not matter.

I desired Megan, regardless of how much Jason fought it.

Chapter 7

Megyn

I felt guilty after Shane's texts.

For some reason, I knew I couldn't stay away from both of them.

I tried to see the logic in Jason's reasoning, but I'm not so sure anymore. I placed my hand on my growing baby bump and smiled. I thought, "twins, I was having twin babies."

I still don't know which billionaire twin was the father, but I didn't care. I knew that there was a 50/50 chance that it could be Hunters or Shane's kid. So it honestly did not matter.

Jason decided to leave town after concluding talks with the VCs. But before he left, he handed me a plane ticket and said, "Here's your airline ticket. I expect you to take the flight home once your finals are over. I will wait for you at the airport over there."

And with that, he left.

Weeks past and the semester came to an end. I was still in my dorm room trying to make a decision.

Karla said her goodbyes. She was off to visit her parents in New York.

She said" I hope everything works out for you."
I smiled back at her and said: "I hope so too."

She nodded and said, "if you ever need anything, just give me a call." I smiled and thanked her.

Then she said: " I will say this one thing, Megyn if you care about Hunter and Shane, you should be with them. Life is too short for regrets. Plus your babies need their dads."

"Thanks," I said.

And with that, she walked out the room. I couldn't believe the semester was already over. With everything going on, I kept my grades up.

I heard a knock on the door.

I wondered who it was.

Without thinking, I opened the door and looked up. Standing at the door was Shane and Hunter.

"What are you doing here? What are you guys doing here?" I beamed, pleased to see them. My heart skipped a beat.

Shane said "you did not think we would let you get away that easily, did you? We love you, Megan, we haven't felt this way about anyone."

Hunter looked down at my bulging belly and placed his hand tenderly on it and said,"My baby."

That's the moment, Shane playfully pushed him aside and said: "It could be mine to it probably is."

I laughed and said, "Well you never know with twins."

They said "You have to come home with us tonight. We missed you we promise nothing would happen. We just want to be around you."

I laughed. Then I thought if all Hunter and Shane knew how much I desired their warm bodies pressed up on mine, they would realize how hoped something would happen.

I said, "I'll get my things."

They said "You don't need anything. We have something special planned for you."

My eyes widened. I asked, "What do you have planned?"

They said, "It's a secret."

And with that Hunter held my right hand and led me to their Mercedes' ultra-luxe G-Wagon .

Shane followed holding onto my luggage. Shane and Hunter got in the front. Shane got in the driver's seat while Hunter sat beside him. I sat behind them.

As we drove down the Bay Area 101 freeway, Shane mentioned they decided to make the area home. The wanted to be with me.

I reminded them about Jason's request to transfer schools. Then I mentioned the one-way airline ticket Jason purchased.

They didn't say a word. Instead, they glanced at each other.

I said, "Are you going to say something? what do you guys
think?"

They said "It's not going to happen you're going to be with us, darling."

And with that moments later, we arrived at a stunning Palo Alto home. I gasped, it was even more significant than the party's mansion.

Shane got out and opened the door to let me out.

I said, "Whose home is this?"

Hunter said: "We just bought it."

Then Shane said

"It's yours. We bought it for you, darling" Then he kissed my lips; I kissed him back.

"You are glowing," he said. Then he added:

"Would you like to see what's inside?"

"I love to, Shane."

Then I turned, and Hunter pulled me into his arms and began planting soft wet kisses on my lips.

He took a nipple into his lips and flicked his tongue around it making me moan out in ecstasy. Then he began flicking and the other one teasing me until I pleaded for him to let me have a taste of his massive cock.

I needed his length sliding inside of my lips. I wanted the two of them to fuck me hard. He stood up and and unbuckled his pants my heart was beating fast.

I got wet from Shane sucking on my pussy.

Fuck yeah Shane moaned between licks.

I want you to come he want you to come hard. Shane said still sucking on my throbbing Clit. My legs begin to quiver. I felt my body pleading for a climax. Hunter kept sucking on my hard sensitive nipples as though his life depended on it. The sounds from their sucking on my large breasts and my wet pulsating nub sent my body reeling in ecstasy.

"Fuck your liquid gold tastes delicious darling," Hunter moaned. He kept sucking on my milk filled ducts while Shane lapped up my intimate juices.

I close my eyes and roll my hips over Shane's lips, his tongue spearing sensually into my pussy. I screamed out : "Here oh, hmm, here I cum". Hunter slipped his lips off my hard nipples. The he whispered into my ears, "Cum darling, the next round is going to be much more exciting baby!" He slammed his lips on mine. Then Hunter continued kneading on my breasts as Shane finger fucked me and flicked his tongue on my clit.

I came hard spilling my juices all over Shane's chin. Shane licked my juices clean. Then he smiled and said, "your orgasm tastes like pure honey, darling!"

Then the next thing I knew, they led me into the mirrored master bedroom. I smiled and stared at my loves with lust in my eyes. Then I turned and notice a leather sex swing in the adjacent room. It brought back memories. Shane smiled and asked if he I wanted to give it a go. I thought about it for a moment.

Then I said, "Hmm maybe next time" They laughed and with a tender hand lifted me up and placed me on the bed. Then I felt Hunter's warm breath on the nape of my neck as he slid my clothes off. Shane undressed and positioned his body on the opposite side of the bed. I turned to face Shane. He gave me a kiss. I kissed him back and then I turned to Hunter and kissed him as well.

Hunter's hands glided along my shoulders and palmed my breasts. *I gasped in pleasure as Hunter twirled my right nipple between his fingers. Then he slid his hands between my thighs flicking his digits on my wet folds. Not to be outdone, Shane lowered his lips on my left breast. He began sucking on my boobs while at the same time, fisting and stroking his large 10 inch cock in the palm of his hand.*

Shane asked "Who do you want first this time darling?" I couldn't decide. I wanted them both so Shane said "Hunter should go first this time around." Hunter smiled and agreed. Hunter began planting wet kisses along my sensitive curves. I moaned, little gasps of delightful pleasure escaped my lips.

Then I watched as Hunger got on his feet, slid his pants down and stroked his cock. A bead of precum dripped out of its delicate tip. I instinctively spread my legs as far apart as I could ready to receive his hardness balls deep in my pussy. Shane's hands slid the hair out of my face giving me a better view. I gasped the moment I felt Hunter's smooth crown nudge at my tight entrance.

"Still so fucking tight and soft darling," Hunter groaned pushing an inch into my wet slit. Hunter stared at me with those dark incredibly sexy eyes of his. He slid my right leg over his shoulder. Then he murmured "I want to watch your face darling as you cum around my cock sweetie."

And with that, he continued thrusting his hardness into my sex. Then he pulled out almost the way.

"Please Hunter don't stop please," I begged pushing my hips to capture his pulsating cock. He said "We have held on this long. I am backed up sweetie, there is is no stopping now."

That is the moment he slammed his entire length deep into my walls coating his shaft with my wetness. I moaned in pleasure rotating my hips in circles around his hard cock. Then suddenly he pulled out almost all the way.

"Hunter please stop teasing me," I pleaded reaching. Hunter did not respond he plunged his entire shaft deep into my pussy. My intimate muscles tightened around his shaft and began milking him. Then I felt Shane nudging my lips with his Cock. Still impaled by Hunters hardness, I turned and took Shane's long slightly slimmer cock into my mouth. My mouth sucked on him desperately seeking the cream that lay inside.

"Hmm good girl, fucking sexy. How did we get this lucky?" Shane purred as I looked up to watch his reaction. He looked satisfied and that pleased me. I kept sucking on Shane's beautiful length while Hunter kept up the pace hammering home.

"Fuck jesus here I cum darling, I am going to cum inside your juicy slit!" Hunter groaned his body tensing up, his pace got faster and harder. I kept bopping my head back and forth over Shane's cock. My toes curled as orgasm after orgasm hit my body sending me into a blissful state. Hunter came with a shuddering cry spilling his cum deep inside my tight soaked walls.

At that moment, Shane growled with pleasure releasing ropes of his cum down my throat. Shane slid out of my lips and Hunter slid his cock out of my core. Shane positioned his cock at my entrance.

He placed his hands underneath my ass. Then he lifted me up slicking his smooth crown up and down my wetness. I watched as he slammed his cock inside my tight cunt. His long throbbing soak filled member plunged balls deep inside my walls. Then our bodies began slamming against each other, skin to skin.

"Oh sweetie you are still so freakin tight! I need to feel you cumming around my dick darling" He purred as my wetness coated up his shaft, spearing him on.

My pussy tightened hard around his shaft keeping him inside and milking him. He lowered his lips on my breasts and sucked one after the other.

Then he moved up to my lips and kissed my lips like a desperate lover. It was not a chaste kiss but one of a man who desired only one woman and that made me smile. I flung my hands around his neck and then dug my finger into his back. Overwhelmed by his massive girth stretching my slit to the hilt, I clutched onto him.

"So wet and tight, I love you with my entire being!" he cried out in ecstasy making every nerve ending in my body quiver.

I grabbed his hair and pulled him close as multiple orgasms tore through my petite body. Shane's throbbing cock kept up the pace racing to an insane climax. Then he flipped my body over so now he had his back on the bed and then he began thrusting up into my pussy. I knew what was coming up next, the thought made my arousal grow and sure enough I felt a finger in my ass then another. It was Hunters.

"Put it in please!Put it darling!" I pleaded. Shane lowered my body to his chest so my ass was pushed up. That is the moment I felt hunter grab my hips in his firm palms and slam his cock into my ass.

"Fuck darling, so tight" he purred. "No woman has ever felt this good wrapped around my cock." He said. Filled once again by my twin lovers, pleasure ripped through my body like a bolt of lightning.

The sound of rain outside the mansion drowned by the sound of sex as our bodies moved in rhythm with each other. Hunter clenched my hair as he pounded his way to an insane climax. Shane then clasped my breasts and twirled my nipples between his fingers.

The sounds of our naked bodies slapping drowned the sound of thunder and rain outside.
"Please be ours darling" Hunter murmured. "Lets come together darling"
And with that I felt their bodies tense up, Hunter clasped my hips and pulled me back for one last savage thrust. I held my breath as his slammed his hardness deep into my A-spot. An incredible feeling of pleasure rocked my body at that

moment. I looked down at Shane, his cock coated in my pussy juices.

"Nngh! here I come darling!" He cried out sitting up and slamming his cock up into my tight wet slit one final time. That is the moment We came at the same time in mutual pleasure. I felt the warmth of their beautiful cum fill me up both ways. Spent we fell onto the bed both men tenderly wrapping their hands on my pregnant belly.

Epilogue

A lot happened since we moved into the mansion; it turns out that realized how much we loved each other. We then decided to embark on an unconventional relationship. Hunter and Shane promised to be with only me, pleasuring and protecting me forever.

I had the twins, and what's incredible was the fact that both Hunter and Shane were biological dads to each twin!

Hunters son came out first, followed by Shanes.

I asked the doctor how it was possible that were both dads at the same time?

The doctor said it's a rare occurrence, but it does happen. He called it superfecundation. We named the twins Ethan and Harry.

As for Jason, he finally came around when he realized he had no choice. For some reason, once he saw his nephews, he realized how much Shane and Hunter loved and treasured me.

They rekindled their unbreakable friendship but Jason jokingly still gave Hunter and Shane a stern warning.

"Break my sister's heart and I will break you two!"

They laughed at the thought and reassured Jason, they would do no such thing!
 I was pleased. Weeks later on the very day the doctor gave the go-ahead to have sex again. Let's just say; I was insatiable that night, and luckily the twins were up to the task, what more could a girl ask for?

The end.

OFF LIMITS DADDY

PART OF THE "BILLIONAIRE SINNERS" SERIES

ANASTASIA SLASH

I again noticed his sexy tribal sleeve tattoo on his arm. Something I secretly found attractive in men. I ran my fingers over it, he smirked and watched my fingers teasing his arm.

'Are you ready darling let's go" he said rising to his feet. I marveled at his height, 6 ft 4! I am petite. Our height difference was incredible, but that did not stop him from wanting me. "I can't wait to have you wet and cumming in the club tonight babe!" He said taking my hand in his and leading me to towards a private room. As we proceeded to the room, I listened to the moaning sounds coming from all around me.

All of the couples were dressed in Halloween costumes. They kept their clothes on as they fucked each other.

I mean it was crazy, a fairy having sex with a ghost?

My masked stranger guided me to the wall, and then he placed his hands between my thighs. His fingers began moving up my inner thighs towards my soaked folds.

I reached over and squeezed his massive

bulge.

Click here to continue reading

Knocked up by the A List

KNOCKED UP BY THE A LIST

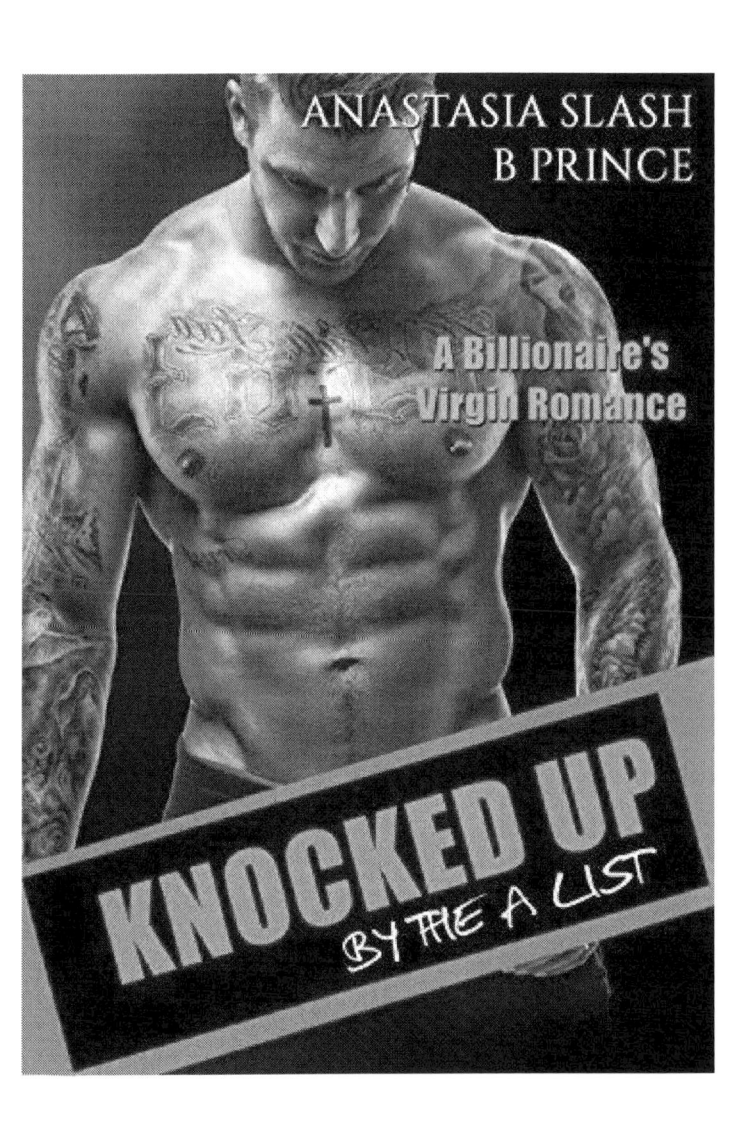

ANASTASIA SLASH B PRINCE

A Billionaire's Virgin Romance

Excerpt!

I closed my eyes feeling his thickness close to my lips.

I wrapped my slender fingers around it and took it all in

This was my first time doing such a thing, but you would never know it.

That's because, thanks to videos and the amazing lectures I got from my girls, using vegetables, I knew what to do.

But then moments later, he pulls me up for a kiss.

He lowered my body down on the bed. We began kissing passionately when I felt him nudging at my entrance and pushing in. Could this be it? But shouldn't we? I didn't care. His actions sent a pleasurable sensation rocketing through my petite body. Fuck! It feels so freaking good. But could I be in for it? Will my actions have consequences?

[Click here to continue reading](#)

Thanks for reading please follow me on [facebook](#). I appreciate it!
And don't forget to check out my other books.

[HERE](#)

Printed in Great Britain
by Amazon